The Crow and the Raven

Why should you be yourself?

www.av2books.com

Go to **www.av2books.com**, and enter this book's unique code.

BOOK CODE

T 5 6 7 8 4 8

AV² by Weigl brings you media enhanced books that support active learning.

Published by AV² by Weigl
350 5th Avenue, 59th Floor New York, NY 10118

Library of Congress Cataloging-in-Publication Data
Fax 1-866-449-3445 For the attention of the Publishing Records department.

ISBN 978-1-62127-916-7 (Hardcover)
ISBN 978-1-48960-130-8 (Multi-user eBook)

Senior Editor: Heather Kissock
Project Coordinator: Alexis Roumanis
Art Director: Terry Paulhus

Printed in the United States in North Mankato, Minnesota
1 2 3 4 5 6 7 8 9 0 17 16 15 14 13

052013
WEP300513

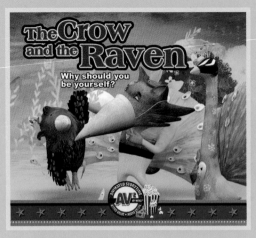

FABLE SYNOPSIS

For thousands of years, parents and teachers have used memorable stories called fables to teach simple moral lessons to children.

In the Aesop's Fables by AV² series, classic fables are given a lighthearted twist. These familiar tales are performed by a troupe of animal players whose endearing personalities bring the stories to life.

In *The Crow and the Raven*, Aesop and his troupe teach their audience about the dangers of trying to be like someone else. They learn that you will make yourself look silly if you try to be something you are not.

This AV² media enhanced book comes alive with...

Animated Video
Watch a custom animated movie.

Try This!
Complete activities and hands-on experiments.

Key Words
Study vocabulary, and complete a matching word activity.

Quiz
Test your knowledge.

The Crow and the Raven

Why should you be yourself?

AV² Storytime Navigation

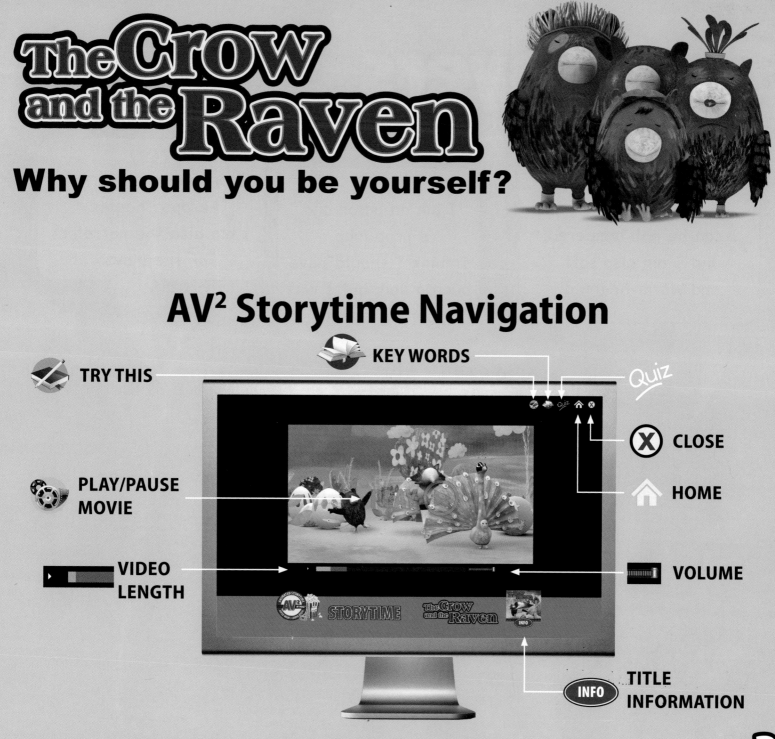

TRY THIS

KEY WORDS

Quiz

CLOSE

PLAY/PAUSE MOVIE

HOME

VIDEO LENGTH

VOLUME

INFO TITLE INFORMATION

The Players

Aesop
I am the leader of Aesop's Theater, a screenwriter, and an actor.
I can be hot-tempered, but I am also soft and warm-hearted.

Libbit
I am an actor and a prop man.
I think I should have been a lion, but I was born a rabbit.

Presy
I am the manager of Aesop's Theater.
I am also the narrator of the plays.

Elvis
I like dance and music. I am artistic. I am very good at drawing.

Bogart
I am the strongest and the oldest pig. I always do whatever I want.

Audrey
I am a very good and caring pig. If someone cries, I cry with them. I never lie.

Milala
I think I am cute. I like to get attention from the other animals.

Goddard
I am very greedy. I like food.

5

The Story

Elvis danced on stage.

"Fa la la! I am the most beautiful peacock in the world."

The audience cheered for Elvis.

"Elvis is the biggest star of my theater!" said Aesop.

After the play ended, the actors gathered together.

"Everyone liked our play," said Aesop. "Good job, Elvis!

I loved how you played the peacock!"

Elvis was not surprised at Aesop's praise.

He knew his performance was very good.

9

Elvis showed Aesop a list.

"I know I am the best actor you have. I should be treated like a star," said Elvis.

Aesop read the list and was surprised.

"You need your own room, bathroom, and a milk bath?" asked Aesop. "You even want me to change the name of my theater to 'Aesop and Elvis' Theater'?"

"I know how amazing I am. If you don't do what I want, I won't sing at the next show," said Elvis.

11

"Why would Elvis think he is better than us?" asked Presy.

"Elvis is not acting like himself," said Aesop.

"Tickets are sold out for tomorrow. What will we do if Elvis doesn't sing? He is the only one who knows the songs," Libbit said nervously.

All of the animals looked worried.

The next morning, Elvis sat at an empty table.

Elvis demanded that he have a special breakfast

"Why do you want to eat alone?" asked Presy.

"Big stars need more space than everyone else," said Elvis.

Presy rolled her eyes and brought Elvis his breakfast.

After breakfast, the actors cleaned up the stage.

Elvis was the only one who did not help.

He announced to the group that he needed to rest

before he went on stage.

"There must be some way we can teach Elvis a lesson.

We are all just as important as he is," said Aesop.

Aesop sat down to write a new play, *The Crow and the Raven*.

"Elvis will play the crow, and I will play the

peacock," said Aesop.

One day, a crow found some peacock feathers.

The crow used the feathers to dress up like a peacock.

The crow's friends thought his new costume was beautiful.

When one of his friends tried to touch the feathers, the crow pushed her back.

"Get away! I'm a peacock, not an ugly crow," said the crow.

"When you are beautiful like me, then we can be friends."

Two peacocks walked towards the crow.

"Hello peacocks! I love how beautiful our feathers are, don't you?" said the crow.

The peacocks agreed with the crow. They admired his feathers as well as their own.

The peacocks bowed to the crow.

The crow was so flattered that he bowed back.

As the crow made his low bow, he tripped and fell over.

All his feathers fell off.

The peacocks were shocked to see a crow.

"You are a crow!" the peacocks yelled. They were very
upset that the crow had lied.

23

The crow was not able to get up.

He asked his friends for help.

"You said that we were ugly," said one.

"You wanted to be a peacock," said another.

"We don't want to play with someone who thinks he is better than us," said a third crow.

The crows flew away, leaving him all alone.

The crow felt bad for thinking he was better than his friends.

He felt silly for pretending to be something he was not.

After the play, Elvis took off his costume.

He was all alone with no one to talk to.

Elvis realized that he was only pretending to be a star.

Everyone had to work together to make the play a

success. Elvis felt bad for treating his friends poorly.

He went to find his friends and tell them he was sorry.

You will make yourself look silly if

you try to be something you are not.

What Is a Story?

Players

Who is the story about? The characters, or players, are the people, animals, or objects that perform the story. Characters have personality traits that contribute to the story. Readers understand how a character fits into the story by what the character says and does, what others say about the character, and how others treat the character.

Setting

Where and when do the events take place? The setting of a story helps readers visualize where and when the story is taking place. These details help to suggest the mood or atmosphere of the story. A setting is usually presented briefly, but it explains whether the story is taking place in the past, present, or future and in a large or small area.

Plot

What happens in the story? The plot is a story's plan of action. Most plots follow a pattern. They begin with an introduction and progress to the rising action of events. The events lead to a climax, which is the most exciting moment in the story. The resolution is the falling action of events. This section ties up loose ends so that readers are not left with unanswered questions. The story ends with a conclusion that brings the events to a close.

Point of View

Who is telling the story? The story is normally told from the point of view of the narrator, or storyteller. The narrator can be a main character or a less important character in the story. He or she can also be someone who is not in the story but is observing the action. This observer may be impartial or someone who knows the thoughts and feelings of the characters. A story can also be told from different points of view.

Dialogue

What type of conversation occurs in the story? Conversation, or dialogue, helps to show what is happening. It also gives information about the characters. The reader can discover what kinds of people they are by the words they say and how they say them. Writers use dialogue to make stories more interesting. In dialogue, writers imitate the way real people speak, so it is written differently than the rest of the story.

Theme

What is the story's underlying meaning? The theme of a story is the topic, idea, or position that the story presents. It is often a general statement about life. Sometimes, the theme is stated clearly. Other times, it is suggested through hints.

The Crow and the Raven Quiz

1
What did Elvis give to Aesop?

2
What did everyone do after breakfast?

3
What was Elvis's role in the play?

4
What made the crow lose his feathers?

5
Why were the peacocks mad at the crow?

6
What lesson did Elvis learn?

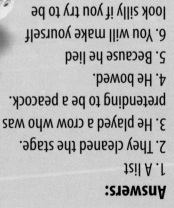

Answers:

1. A list
2. They cleaned the stage.
3. He played a crow who was pretending to be a peacock.
4. He bowed.
5. Because he lied
6. You will make yourself look silly if you try to be something you are not.

Key Words

Research has shown that as much as 65 percent of all written material published in English is made up of 300 words. These 300 words cannot be taught using pictures or learned by sounding them out. They must be recognized by sight. This book contains 133 common sight words to help young readers improve their reading fluency and comprehension. This book also teaches young readers several important content words, such as proper nouns. These words are paired with pictures to aid in learning and improve understanding.

Page	Sight Words First Appearance
4	a, also, am, an, and, be, been, but, can, have, I, man, of, plays, should, the, think, was
5	always, animals, at, do, food, from, get, good, if, like, never, other, them, to, very, want, with
6	for, in, is, most, my, on, said, story, world
8	after, he, his, how, not, our, together, you
10	asked, change, don't, even, know, list, me, name, need, next, own, read, show, what, your
13	all, are, one, only, out, than, us, we, who, why, will, would
14	big, eat, eyes, her, more, that
16	before, did, group, help, up, went
17	as, down, important, just, must, new, some, there, way, write
19	away, back, day, found, then, thought, used, when
20	so, their, they, two, walked, well
22	had, made, off, over, see, were
24	another, him, something
26	find, look, make, no, talk, tell, took, try, work

Page	Content Words First Appearance
4	actor, leader, lion, manager, narrator, rabbit, screenwriter, theater
5	attention, dance, music, pig
6	audience, peacock, stage, star
8	job, performance, praise
10	bath, bathroom, milk, room
13	songs, tickets
14	breakfast, morning, space, table
17	crow, lesson, raven
19	costume, feathers, friends
26	success

Check out av2books.com for your animated storytime media enhanced book!

1 Go to av2books.com

2 Enter book code | T 5 6 7 8 4 8

3 Fuel your imagination online!

www.av2books.com

AV² Storytime Navigation

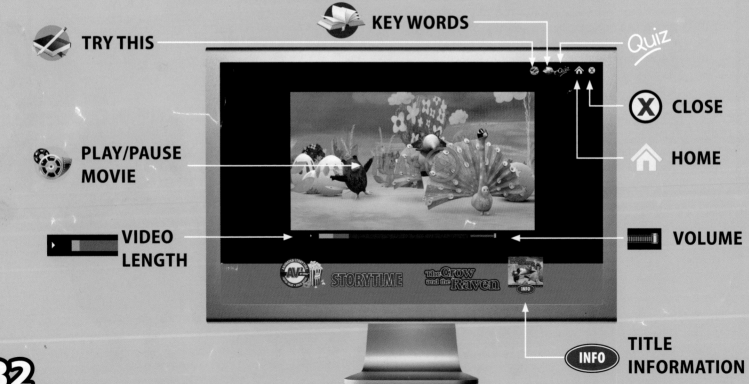

KEY WORDS

TRY THIS

Quiz

X CLOSE

PLAY/PAUSE MOVIE

HOME

VIDEO LENGTH

VOLUME

INFO **TITLE INFORMATION**